SOMETHING SPECIAL
FOR MISS MARGERY

WRITTEN BY JANET SLATER REDHEAD ILLUSTRATED BY IAN FORSS

Beethoven was an extremely musical canary.
He sang and whistled beautifully.
He also composed his own songs,
mostly for Miss Margery,
who lived with him.

She would often say, "Beethoven,
you are an extremely musical canary."

Beethoven thought that Miss Margery
was a very wise woman.

Sometimes, in the evenings,
Miss Margery would play the piano,
and Beethoven would sing.

Sometimes Beethoven would whistle
toe-teasing tunes,
and Miss Margery would dance.

Often they would just sit quietly,
listening to records,
sipping their dandelion tea,
and nibbling poppyseed cake.

For Miss Margery's seventieth birthday,
Beethoven decided to compose
an especially happy tune — something so happy,
hand-clappy,
toe-tappy,
song-singy,
leg-springy,
arm-flingy,
that it would make Miss Margery feel
as happy as a birthday every time she heard it.
After all, Miss Margery did a lot
to make life happy for him.

As Beethoven sat thinking
about some of the things
Miss Margery did for him,
a melody just sprang into his beak.

It took him completely by surprise.
The melody was so wonderful that Beethoven
couldn't stop singing it over and over.

It was good that Miss Margery
was at the dentist,
or she would have heard her present
the day before her birthday.

As the mail person put letters
in Miss Margery's mailbox,
he heard Beethoven's song.

"That's a great little tune," he smiled.
He whistled it as he biked on.

A lady, on her way to the supermarket, heard the mail person whistling Beethoven's song.

"That's a great little tune," she smiled. She hummed it as she trundled her trolley around the supermarket.

A man, who played the saxophone in a restaurant, heard the lady humming Beethoven's song in the supermarket.

"That's a great little tune," he smiled.
He hurried home to practice it on his saxophone so he could play it in the restaurant.

That evening, Miss Margery seemed unusually sad for a person with a birthday the next day. She ate her poppyseed cake as if it was the last piece she would ever eat.

"The dentist told me
he's going to pull out my teeth
and make me false ones," she sighed.

"I shall have to give up eating poppyseed cake.
People say you can't manage seeds
with false teeth."

Beethoven was startled.
False teeth! No poppyseed cake!
He wondered if he would ever come
to a time in his life
when he needed a false beak.

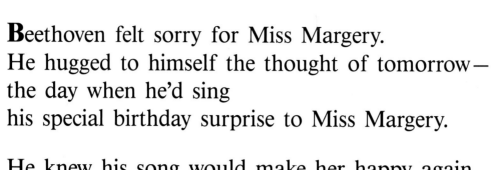

Beethoven felt sorry for Miss Margery.
He hugged to himself the thought of tomorrow—
the day when he'd sing
his special birthday surprise to Miss Margery.

He knew his song would make her happy again.

That very same night,
the man with the saxophone
played the tune in the restaurant.

Some people from a record company
heard the tune.

"That's a great little tune," they smiled.
"We must make that into a record."

When Miss Margery woke up next morning,
she was still miserable.
It almost made Beethoven weep
to see her so sad on her birthday—
the very day she should be so happy.

"I'll soon change this!" he thought.
He opened his beak to sing her
his special birthday surprise.

But it was Beethoven's turn to be surprised.
Instead of the happy birthday song,
Beethoven found himself singing a tune
so sad and gloomy,
that even the flowers in the vase
drooped their heads.

No matter how he tried,
Beethoven was unable to sing one happy note.

The sadder Miss Margery became,
the sadder Beethoven's songs became.

And the sadder his songs became,
the sadder Miss Margery became.

As the days went by,
Miss Margery and Beethoven grew more
and more miserable.
They'd almost forgotten what it was like
to be happy.

'If only I could remember my tune!'
thought Beethoven.

On the day Miss Margery had to pick up
her new false teeth from the dentist,
she stopped at a record store.

"I need some music to brighten me up," she said.
"I'm even making my canary miserable."

"I've got the perfect record for you
and your canary, Madam," smiled the storekeeper.
"This will have you singing in the shower
before you've turned the water on."

That evening, Miss Margery cut
a slice of poppyseed cake for Beethoven,
a slice of sponge cake for herself,
poured out the dandelion tea,
and switched on the record player.
Beethoven nearly choked on a seed.

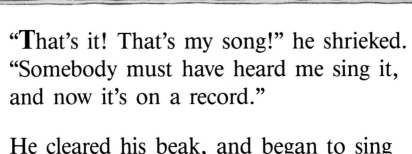

"That's it! That's my song!" he shrieked.
"Somebody must have heard me sing it,
and now it's on a record."

He cleared his beak, and began to sing
as he had never sung before.

"**O**h, Beethoven," cried Miss Margery.
"I've never heard a tune so happy,
hand-clappy,
toe-tappy,
song-singy,
leg-springy,
arm-flingy.
You are an extremely musical and clever canary."

Then Miss Margery tucked up her skirt,
and began to dance and prance,
and skip and flip,
and toe-tap and hand-clap,
and sing and spring and fling,
and behave like a person with
all of their birthdays wrapped up into one.

The happier Miss Margery became,
the happier Beethoven's song became.

The happier his song became,
the happier Miss Margery became.

Now that Beethoven had remembered
his special tune,
and Miss Margery had remembered
how to be happy,
they didn't need a record any more.
They were as happy as a birthday,
every day after!